For my precious son, Rohan

All You Need Is Love

Celebrating Families of All Shapes and Sizes

Shanni Collins

Jessica Kingsley Publishers
London and Philadelphia

*The author and publisher would like to acknowledge
Sarah Brice for her input with the design of this book.*

First published in 2017
by Jessica Kingsley Publishers
73 Collier Street
London N1 9BE, UK
and
400 Market Street, Suite 400
Philadelphia, PA 19106, USA

www.jkp.com

Library of Congress Cataloging in Publication Data
A CIP catalog record for this book is available from the Library of Congress

British Library Cataloguing in Publication Data
A CIP catalogue record for this book is available from the British Library

ISBN 978 1 78592 251 0
eISBN 978 1 78450 534 9

6-18

Printed and bound in China

Contents

Guide for Supporting Adults
by Pooky Knightsmith • 30

Acknowledgements • 34

One of a Kind

Our daughter is amazing, she's one of a kind.

She has Down's syndrome and a beautiful mind.

Her heart and her soul are as big as the moon

and she brightens the world, like a flower in bloom!

Singing is something we both love to do.

I use a hairbrush; she sometimes does too.

We're good at chatting, about worries, this and that,

and if it feels really big, we both wear a hat.

We learn from each other, we jump over puddles,

hands held together, and long warming cuddles.

Our spotty umbrellas bring glances our way.

It's me and my daughter, I'm SO proud to say.

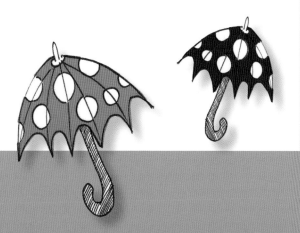

Weekend Dads

At weekends, I love to go down to the sea
to spend time with the men who foster me.
We run in the woods, with the dogs, through the trees,
and stop at the cafe for toast with melted cheese.

The men I call dads are amazing and kind;
they help with my homework and don't seem to mind.
When I'm grumpy and tired and I just want to sleep,
they let me be me, and then I'm back on my feet!

We do jigsaws, play football, go shopping for clothes.
Xbox with Jamie, whilst Jim has a doze.
There's friends all around and I love my sea home,
the dogs and the dads and my new mobile phone!

My Hairy Sister

My family is me and my mums, which is cool.
I love my friends coming round after school.
We play in the garden, do Swingball and bounces.
Trampolining's so good; we can jump, high as houses!

I was born from a seed that a nice man donated
and my mums planted it, so that I'd be created.
We talk and we're open with no words unspoken,
and I've known from the start, what goes on in my heart.

Our dog is a friend who I call 'hairy sister'
and I love her so much, I like to sit with her.
With her waggly tale, I've a friend by my side.
She's always so happy, which fills me with pride!

My family is fun and a little bit bonkers,
with grandads and nanas and cousins and aunties.
We dance in the kitchen, read stories at night,
go walking in wellies; my life feels just right!

Our Dad Is Poorly

Our dad, he likes telly and loves watching sports.

He played Sunday rugby, wearing bright shorts.

We love to dress up, the more funny the better.

When we're being silly, we have the best times together.

There's me and my brother, and Teddy the bulldog.

Our mum is our leader, who makes life not seem odd.

When sometimes there's stares and people are unsure,

she hugs and explains: That's what mums are for.

Dad is so poorly, it makes him all twitchy.

His legs jump about, and you'd think he was itchy.

He loves telling stories of aliens and mystery

and we all like to listen when he talks about history.

My dad used to fish and spend hours by the river.

He'd win competitions, then bring chips for our dinner.

My family is solid, real gems through and through,

strong for the future, tough as superglue.

My Daughter's a Boy

My baby was born a handsome girl.
She had sparkly eyes and one cheeky curl.
Her smile was a picture that brought tears to our eyes,
of freedom and adventure. She was unique, we realise.

Growing up, she did remarkable things:
stick drumming with twigs, wearing unicorn wings.
She took such pleasure in a fantastical world.
Pure, open and fun was our little girl.

Once older and bolder, a sadness appeared
of thoughts unexplained, and feelings that reared.
The body that grew didn't quite find a place.
For my wonderful person, didn't feel safe.

As a family we listened, we talked and we wept,
then we hugged all together, with not one regret.
Relief came upon us, when his face filled with glee.
Our daughter's a boy, and we'll love him as he.

Me and My Brother

Mummy and Daddy couldn't make a baby
so they adopted my brother from another lady.
Whilst waiting for papers and lots to do,
Mum became pregnant, and then there were two!

When my brother arrived, I was still growing inside,
so she was pushing a pram whilst her tummy was wide.
Then soon after that, I was born in the spring
and me and my brother were nearly a twin!

We loved hearing the story of our family tree,
snuggled up to Mum, both on her knee.
My brother and I are truly adored.
Life's wonder and joy our journeys explored.

My Grandparents

Granny and Grandad are my mum and dad.

Our parents, they died. We were all SO sad.

We weren't really sure how we would cope,

but the love we all felt gave us strength and hope.

Our grandad is funny. He's so good at jokes.

He smells of tobacco but no longer smokes.

When problems arise, he's a good one to ask

then he'll pass us the trowel and sing songs of the past.

Granny is Mum. She's as strong as a bison.

Bakes cakes that are tasty, with thick gooey icing.

She cycles her bike and we follow in tow,

and they teach us great things that help us to grow.

We all often think of our dad and our mum

and at times we remember their love and the fun.

We're so lucky too, to be part of a gang.

Our grandparents are perfect and part of life's plan.

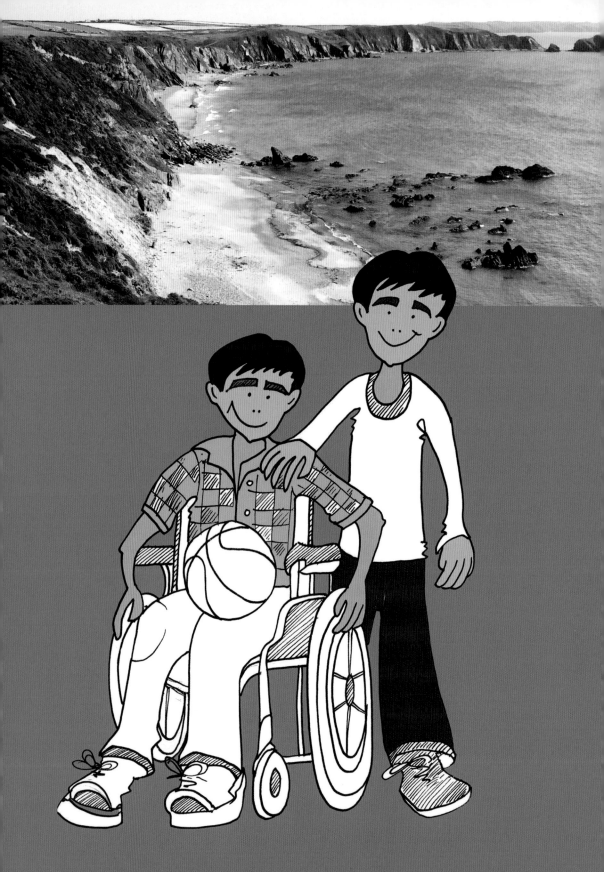

My Twin

We dreamt last night that we flew like a swan,
had the voice of a sky lark that burst into song.
We bounced off the clouds, then dived into the ocean,
swam alongside the fish, filled with their motion.

As we moved through the water, our legs became fins,
whilst sailing the skies, our arms produced wings.
Our thoughts were filled up, with ideas of play
whilst our hearts beat together, in a fun kind of way.

My brother stands by me, as I sit beside him.
We face life together, bright eyes and big grin.
Today we'll adventure, and discover new ways,
creating each moment, embracing our days.

26

Mummy, Daddy and Me

My daddy has skin that is pink with small freckles
And Mummy's big eyes shine bright through her spectacles.
Her face is rich brown, like a cup of smooth coffee
and mine more like sweets, the colour of toffee.

My dad comes from Scotland, high up in the mountains
where carpets of heather appear under fountains.
Mum's family was born in a country of heat,
where mangos grow freely and taste oh so sweet!

She shares many stories that light up her face,
and I listen and long to go back to that place.
I'm grateful because of my parents' traditions,
like singing and drumming and bagpipes in mittens.

People we meet are surprised when they see
that my daddy has skin that is different from me.
So I share, and we talk, of the lands we're all from
and I know that it's perfect. I truly belong.

Your Family

Love is what matters, it's warm like the sun.
Take time to notice your people, one by one:
an auntie, a dog, a friend or a cat.
Having someone who loves you, it's as simple as that.

Families come in all colours, shapes and sizes.
To recognise that, do you know what the prize is?
It's love and acceptance, ease, peace of mind.
Let's celebrate that – and always be kind.

Kindness is great, it helps you and me.
It grows and it blossoms, like flowers on a tree.
Let's hold hands together, and feel our own worth,
spreading love, right round the earth.

All You Need Is Love takes a wonderfully upbeat and fun look at a wide range of different types of family. As well as an uplifting read in its own right, it can provide a great way to discuss a range of different issues, either one-to-one or in a classroom setting.

Exploring the concept of family

Importantly, *All You Need Is Love* celebrates difference and will help children from a variety of family set-ups feel validated and more confident and proud to talk about their family. A great way to encourage this can be to have an open discussion around the word 'family' and what this actually means. You could:

- Explore what a 'typical family' has looked like through the ages, and in different cultures today – is there really any such thing as a typical family at all?

- Think about less-typical families represented in books and television programmes that children have enjoyed (you may need to do your homework on this one as there is not always a great deal of diversity represented in mainstream media, though this is improving).

- Discuss the different families in the book – what is different about them and what is similar? What important things do many families seem to have in common?

- Draw pictures of a range of different types of family – how many different types can you think of?

- You could use these pictures to create a whole class display – perhaps with a range of different family set-ups as the perimeter of a display board, with the qualities that families share (such as love and supporting each other) represented in the middle.

Using specific families to support a child

Reading about a family who is similar to theirs can be deeply reassuring for a child. If a child you're supporting especially identifies with one of the families in the book, you could develop the conversation in a variety of ways:

- Ask the child open-ended questions to encourage them to explore this family and their own – your main role here is to listen whilst they talk.

- Support the child to write a poem about their own family in a similar style to the poems in the book. The poems are quite short so you have to think carefully about the most important things to include, which can be a great chance to talk to the child you're supporting about what makes their family special and wonderful to feel a part of.

- You could tell stories about a family in the book. You could take relatively typical activities, like going shopping, a day at the beach or a day at home, and talk about what sorts of things might happen in this family – are there good bits and less good bits?

- As an extension of the story-telling activity, you could find or make toys to represent a family and act out the stories you tell – you could even film them if you were feeling adventurous!

Safe and sensitive handling of tricky topics

- Whether you're working as a class or one-to-one, some children will be more open to discussion than others. 'Doing' activities such as drawing and crafting can often be a great way to get kids talking – the conversation may well flow as they cut and stick.

- Whilst we'd love every child to feel confident celebrating their family within the classroom, if a child does not want to discuss their family in front of their peers they should not be made too. Do, however, find time to have a discussion with the child to see if there is anything they'd like to explore one-to-one – the book can be a great prompt for discussion.

- Some children may have very set ideas about what family means before you open the discussion; be prepared for this and understand that it can take a little time to expand horizons.

Most importantly, have fun with the child or children you're supporting and encourage them to celebrate the things that make their family special. No two families are quite the same, after all!

Acknowledgements

I'm so grateful to all of the wonderful people in my life who have given me the inspiration to create this book.

Be big, bold and beautiful.

Shanni

Shanni Collins went to art college and trained in theatre design. She loves to climb mountains and play beach volleyball. Shanni has a remarkable family and lives in Brighton with her son, Rohan, and dog, Pepper.

Contact: shanni.collins@mac.com

Dr Pooky Knightsmith is a specialist in child and adolescent mental health and emotional wellbeing. She is the director of the children young people and schools' programme at the Charlie Waller Memorial Trust. Pooky has a wonderful family; she lives in a bungalow with her two daughters – one who grew in her tummy and one who didn't – as well as a cat, a dog and her husband. Her daughters' granny and grandad live in the house next door!

of related interest

Something Different About Dad
How to Live with Your Amazing Asperger Parent
Kirsti Evans and John Swogger
Illustrated by John Swogger
ISBN 978 1 78592 012 7
eISBN 978 1 78450 259 1

Can I tell you about Gender Diversity?
A guide for friends, family and professionals
CJ Atkinson
Illustrated by Olly Pike
ISBN 978 1 78592 105 6
eISBN 978 1 78450 367 3

Your Body is Awesome
Body Respect for Children
Sigrun Danielsdottir
Illustrated by Bjork Bjarkdottir
ISBN 978 1 84819 228 7
eISBN 978 0 85701 178 7